Pooh's Honey Tree

Disney's
Winnie the Pooh First Readers

Disney's

A Winnie the Pooh First Reader

Pooh's Honey Tree

Adapted by Isabel Gaines

ILLUSTRATED BY Nancy Stevenson

Disney
PRESS

NEW YORK

Pooh's
Honey Tree

Winnie the Pooh

was a bear of little brain.

But he had a big,

loving heart.

And a big,

round tummy.

Pooh's tummy always looked

quite full.

But it always felt

quite hungry.

Hungry for honey!

One day Pooh went

to the cupboard

and got out his honeypot.

There was nothing left

but the sticky part.

Suddenly, Pooh heard

a buzzing sound.

BUZZ! BUZZ! BUZZ!

"That buzzing means something,"

said Pooh.

Something small and fuzzy

flew past his ear.

BUZZ! BUZZ! BUZZ!

"Oh!" said Pooh. "A bee!"

Now, it is true

that Pooh was not very smart.

But one thing he knew:

where there are bees,

there is honey!

So . . .

Pooh followed the bee

deep into the Hundred-Acre

Wood.

Soon they came

to a tall, tall tree.

A honey tree!

Up the tree Pooh went.

Up.

Up.

Up.

Then, CRACK!

A branch broke.

Down the tree Pooh fell.

Down.

Down.

Down.

Pooh rubbed his sore head.

All that head-rubbing

made Pooh think.

And the first thing he thought of

was Christopher Robin.

Pooh picked himself up

and set off to find

his friend.

When Pooh got

to Christopher Robin's house

he looked

at Christopher Robin's bike.

A big blue balloon was tied

to it.

"May I borrow your balloon?"

Pooh asked Christopher Robin.

"I need it to get some honey."

Christopher Robin gave Pooh

the balloon.

"Here, Pooh.

But you can't get honey

with a balloon," he said.

"Oh, yes, I can," said Pooh.

"I will hang on to the string

and float up to the honey."

20

"Silly old bear," said
Christopher Robin.
"The bees will see you.
They will not let you near
their honey."
"Yes, they will," Pooh said.

Pooh and Christopher Robin

went back

to Pooh's honey tree.

Next, Pooh sat down

in the mud and rolled around.

Soon he was covered

with mud from his nose

to his toes.

"Look!" Pooh said.

"The bees will think

I'm a little black rain cloud.

They will not even know

I am there."

"Oh," said Christopher Robin.

He sat down

under the honey tree

to see what would

happen next.

Pooh held on tight

to the big blue balloon.

Then he floated

all the way up

to the top of the tree.

Pooh tried to act

like a little black rain cloud.

He hung by the tree

for a long, long time.

Then he reached

into the hole

and pulled out a pawful

of golden honey.

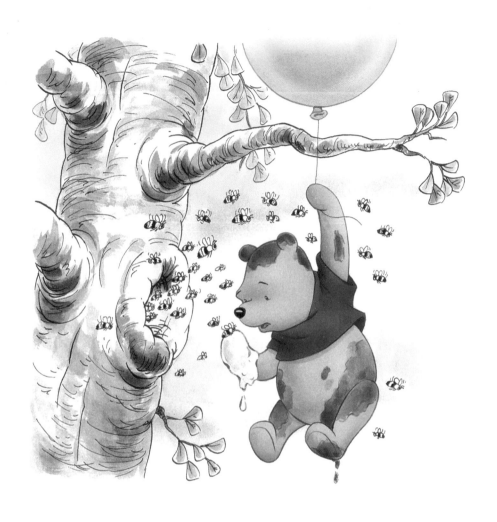

BUZZ! BUZZ! BUZZ!

The bees began to buzz

around Pooh's head.

They were not fooled at all.

All of a sudden,

the balloon string

came undone.

Pooh hopped onto the balloon

before it could get away.

Then Pooh and his balloon

sailed over the treetops.

Then the balloon

lost all its air.

Down it came.

And down came Pooh.

This time, Pooh landed

right on top

of Christopher Robin.

Pooh looked up at the bees
in the tree.
Then he looked down
at Christopher Robin.
"Oh dear!" Pooh said.
"I guess it all comes
from liking honey so much!"

Join the Pooh Friendship Club!

A wonder-filled year of friendly activities and interactive fun for your child!

The fun starts with:
- Clubhouse play kit
- Exclusive club T-shirt
- The first issue of "Pooh News"
- Toys, stickers and gifts from Pooh

The fun goes on with:
- Quarterly issues of "Pooh News" each with special surprises
- Birthday and Friendship Day cards from Pooh
- And more!

Join now and also get a colorful, collectible Pooh art print

Yearly membership costs just $25 plus 15 Hunny Pot Points. (Look for Hunny Pot Points **3** on Pooh products.)

To join, send check or money order and Hunny Pot Points to:

Pooh Friendship Club
P.O. Box 1723
Minneapolis, MN 55440-1723

Please include the following information: Parent name, child name, complete address, phone number, sex (M/F), child's birthday, and child's T-shirt size (S, M, L)
(CA and MN residents add applicable sales tax.)

Call toll-free for more information
1-888-FRNDCLB

You're a Real Friend

Fun for kids ages 3-8!

Pooh Friendship Club

Pooh

Help your child learn
MATH and READING
with a computer and
a silly old bear.

©Disney

 Learning Series on CD-ROM

Put your child on the path to success in the 100 Acre Wood, where Pooh and his friends make learning math and reading fun. Disney's Ready for Math with Pooh helps kids learn all the important basics, including patterns, sequencing, counting, and beginning addition & subtraction. In Disney's Ready to Read with Pooh, kids learn all the fundamentals including the alphabet, phonics, and spelling simple words. Filled with engaging activities and rich learning environments, the 100 Acre Wood is a delightful world for your child to explore over and over. Discover the magic of learning with Pooh.

NEW! Disney's Learning Series

Once Again The Magic Of Disney Begins With a Mouse

Disney INTER ACTIVE

Wonderfully Whimsical Ways To Bring Winnie The Pooh Into Your Child's Life.

Pooh FRIENDSHIP

Pooh and the gang help children learn about liking each other for who they are in 5 charming volumes about what it means to be a friend.

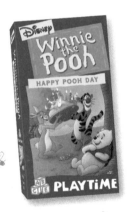

Pooh STORYBOOK CLASSICS

Pooh PLAYTIME

Pooh LEARNING

These 4 enchanting volumes let you share the original A.A. Milne stories — first shown in theaters — you so fondly remember from your own childhood.

Children can't help but play and pretend with Pooh and his friends in 5 playful volumes that celebrate the joys of being young.

Pooh and his pals help children discover sharing and caring in 5 loving volumes about growing up.

FREE*
Flash Cards Attached!
A Different Set With Each *Pooh Learning* Video!
* With purchase, while supplies last.

Printed in U.S.A. © Disney Enterprises, Inc.